D1371869

Bobby and Mandee's
Too Smart For Bullies

by
Deputy Sheriff Robert Kahn
and Sharon Chandler

Illustrated by
Sue Lynn Cotton

**All marketing and publishing rights
guaranteed to and reserved by**

FUTURE HORIZONS INC.

Future Horizons, Inc.
721 W. Abram Street
Arlington, Texas 76013

800-489-0727
 817-277-0727
817-277-2270 fax

Website: www.FutureHorizons-autism.com
E-mail: info@FutureHorizons-autism.com

ISBN #1-885477-76-7

DEDICATION
I wish to thank my family and friends for all of their
support with this book. Especially Lizzy Shannon and
my good friend Dalton LaRue.

Robert Kahn

Hello! My name is Bobby, and this is my sister
Mandee. We are going to tell you about
BULLIES. What is a bully? A bully is someone
who is mean or hurts other people.

Hello, Mandee, how was swimming at the public pool?

It was fine, but something happened on the way home and I need to talk to you.

Tell me what happened, Mandee.

I was walking home and a boy across the street started yelling at me. It was Dalton, a boy I've seen at our school.

Next, Dalton walked across the street and came up to me.

He grabbed me and said, "Give me your money or I will beat you up!"

I got so scared that I started crying. Dalton laughed and then he punched me.

What made it even worse was that other children were gathering around and they started making fun of me.

    I started crying harder and I gave Dalton the money I had.

    He let me go but he said, "Next time, you better have more money for me. Remember also, you better not tell anyone about this or I'm really going to hurt you."

I ran as fast as I could because I just wanted to get away. I was so embarrassed and I felt just awful about myself.

Now that I'm home, I don't want to leave the house ever again.

Mandee, I'm sorry this happened to you, but you can't be afraid to leave our house. Let's work on finding answers to this situation with Dalton.

Bullies like Dalton want to intimidate. This means to make you afraid of them. It is hard not to be intimidated by someone who scares you. Also, they may hurt you because they are usually bigger than you are.

Bullies usually pick on children who are younger, weaker or smaller than they are. This makes the bully feel bigger and more important. If something isn't done to help you, the bully will continue to intimidate and make you feel bad about yourself.

One reason a child is a bully is because someone is being a bully to them. It could be their father, mother, older brother or sister, or someone who lives with them in their house.

The bully feels important by being a bully to other children. This isn't cool and unfortunately, nice children are the ones they pick on.

A bully won't just go away. There are some basic rules when a bully is picking on you. The first one is: you need to tell someone who will help you. THIS IS NOT A SECRET TO BE KEPT. You need to talk to someone because this is a big problem that you cannot solve by yourself. With the help of an adult, there are solutions to this problem.

If the adult you talk to won't listen, then keep telling adults until one of them will listen. REMEMBER, this is a serious problem that you're having and YOU NEED HELP. People you can talk to at home are Parents, Grandparents, Aunts, Uncles, or Trusted Adult Friends.

At school you can talk to Teachers, Principals, Counselors, Secretaries, Aides, Recess Duty People, Librarians, Lunch Room Staff, and the Custodians.

Other grownups you can talk to are a Priest, Minister, Rabbi, Sunday School Teacher, Scout Leader, Coaches, and Police Officers or Deputy Sheriffs.

An adult needs to talk to the bully's parent. If this doesn't work and the bully keeps bothering you, you need to make a police report. Most states have laws which will protect children from bullies. REMEMBER, every child has the right to be safe.

Always try to go places with a friend, or friends, and try not to be alone. Bullies usually won't bother you if you are with other people because your friends will protect you.

Another technique is to avoid the places where the bully hangs out. This is just being smart and safe.

   If the bully confronts you, don't get mad or lose your temper. This is what the bully wants you to do. When you're mad, you're not thinking very well and the bully can start a fight. If this happens, you will probably get hurt.

   Try to say something like, "Please don't" and walk away, or run away. Then go tell a trusted adult immediately.

Mandee, let's go and tell this problem to Mom and Dad. They will make sure you're safe and not afraid to leave our house.

Here is a list of grown-ups, both men and women, who will help you if there is an emergency:

1. Police
2. Sheriff
3. Highway or State Patrol
4. Ambulance drivers
5. Fire fighters
6. Forest rangers
7. Teachers, principals, secretaries, and janitors at a school
8. Postal workers on the job
9. Store clerks on the job
10. Telephone workers (Make sure their truck is with them and that it says phone company on it.)
11. Power company workers (Again, look for the truck.)
12. Garage mechanics on the job

Do you know how to check for an Emergency Vehicle (Police, Fire, and Ambulance) if you have an emergency? Look for at least one red light on the roof of the vehicle.

BOBBY & MANDEE'S SAFETY TEST

We hope you learned about being too smart for bullies. Here is a chance to see how much you learned. Ask your parent or teacher to help you with these questions.

1. How did Mandee feel after Dalton bullied her?
    (answer on page 9)

2. Who is a bully?
    (answer on page 10)

3. What does the word intimidate mean?
    (answer on page 10)

4. Who do bullies usually pick on?
    (answer on page 10)

5. Why is it important to tell someone if a bully is bothering you?
    (answer on page 12)

6. If a bully is bothering you at school, who can you talk to?
    (answer on page 14)

7. Is it against the law to be a bully in most of the United States?
    (answer on page 16)

8. Why should you always walk places with friends and not alone?
    (answer on page 17)

9. What is another way to avoid being bullied?
    (answer on page 17)

10. Why is it important to stay cool when confronted by a bully?
    (answer on page 18)

11. Why should you walk away when confronted by a bully?
    (answer on page 18)

12. Who is Mandee going to talk to about her problem with Dalton?
    (answer on page 19)

911 TIPS FOR PARENTS:

1. Teach your children how to dial 911. A call to 911 should always be a call for help. A call to 911 from a pay phone is free.

Do your children know when to call 911?

- If someone is injured or sick
- If there is smoke or flames in the house
- If they are home alone and someone is trying to get in
- If a stranger follows them home from school
- If they see a car accident
- If they observe someone being hurt by another person
- If during a storm, they see a power pole or another object struck by lightning

Do your children know when NOT to call 911?

- Never call 911 as a joke!
- Never call 911 just for information
- Never call 911 just to see if it works!

2. Be sure to stress the following two points with your child:

- NEVER get into a car with someone unless your parents know you're going with that person
- ALWAYS tell your parents where you're going

OTHER IMPORTANT INFORMATION:

Children need to know their address, phone number, and the type of emergency help they need.

Address _____

Phone _____

Police _____

Fire _____

Medical _____

My List of Safe Grown-ups to Call

_____   _____

_____   _____

_____   _____

_____   _____

_____   _____

_____   _____

Color me!

Mandee and I hope that you learned about BULLIES by reading our book. Watch for our future books about being safe.